THE RIVELIN WRITERS

– VOLUME ONE

EDITED BY ADRIAN G R SCOTT

authorHOUSE®

AuthorHouse™ UK
1663 Liberty Drive
Bloomington, IN 47403 USA
www.authorhouse.co.uk
Phone: 0800.197.4150

Published by AuthorHouse 01/28/2016

ISBN: 978-1-5049-9855-0 (sc)
ISBN: 978-1-5049-9856-7 (e)

Print information available on the last page.

Contents

Preface

In 2011, I was asked to run a writing workshop at a local festival. I had just turned fifty and published a collection of fifty poems to mark the event. Only in the preceding couple of years had I really knuckled down to taking my own work seriously and only hesitantly referred to myself as a poet. I put it this way in a poem written after visiting Dylan Thomas' Welsh home of Laugharne:

'Now in my dog-eared years, signed
up late for pen to paper shoveling'.

This shoveling had met with a degree of success in readership and book sales. It had brought me, somehow, to the attention of a local organizer of the Crosspool Festival, just up the valley from me in Sheffield. I made clear my lack of experience leading writing workshops, she persuasively answered: *'well, you have managed to write and publish and reach people like me, so why not?'* I reluctantly agreed and was somewhat surprised to greet the fourteen folk that turned up to Tapton United Reformed Church Hall: a wonderfully mixed group, octogenarians, a young woman in her twenties, all with some harboured and some tentatively penned, yearnings to write.

I launched into my mix of outwardly impetuous, yet inwardly thinking *'who are you kidding'* spiel. To my amazement I was taken at face value and seriously. Afterwards, a brave lady read me her vulnerable and poignant tribute to her recently departed husband. We were suddenly by the grave together and that night the tender ink of her writing made my tears flow.

'That was great', my host Lesley said; *'please will you run a series of workshops at the Montgomery Theatre in the City Centre,*

where I work?' I agreed on the crest of the evening's wave. After a few sessions, sporadically yet faithfully attended, it became apparent we needed a more conducive, intimate venue. I offered my study/ office housed in a double garage, a book-lined and arm-chaired space with flowing tea and coffee. We decamped and grew, regularly seven souls finding their feet as writers.

I established some ground rules - to listen to the piece with emotional openness and then share what moved you. My own experience was that sharing one's writing is so intimate it needs a warm incubator in which to safely develop. Then, to gently ask questions as to what was being attempted by the linguistic high wire walk and offer possibilities as to how that can be traversed with more balance. All capped with a second reading. Two hours, seven pieces, topped and tailed by my contributions, mainly poems, mine or other writers. Themes were chosen: intimacy, secrets, treasure usually suggested by the interchanges of the group.

More asked to join and this increased the size of the group beyond that which our time and listening capacity could allow. So a second group was born. This followed the same ground rules but chose not to have themes, just to bring a recent piece. In both groups, the prose and poetry interchange was humorous, moving, sparse, verbose and always engaging. There is a wonderful sense of commonplace revelation, we laugh, sigh, gulp back a sob, smile knowingly, and feel we have, more than anything, conversed.

Invariably, when my wife asked me 'how was it?' I would reply, 'wonderful'. I come away from both the groups, meeting every six weeks or so, feeling cultivated, that I had planted some seeds and that many things had germinated in me, that would sprout and flourish in the ordinary allotment of my daily round.

It is in that spirit these pages are offered. It seemed a good thing to share the fruits of our labours, a bit like the village harvest show. All these things that have been grown and cultivated in the secret soil of our quiet journeys, then produced in the groups when almost ripe, we now present to a wider audience in their mellow maturity.

Adrian G R Scott- Winter 2015

We Find Each Other

For the Wedding of Patrick and Sarah July 2014

Miraculously, we find each other, ordinarily
in the mist of the mundane a bond is found,
hands clasp across an uncharted hinterland
and kisses, those rudimentary brokers of connection
fashion the intertwining topiary of two lives
growing together, two families colliding.

Out of a myriad of prospects comes that one face
in whose lineage of laughter lines and tear tracks
your future topography is traced and charted.
Faith in the welding of your two metals into one
seraphic alloy is born and the heated ache of urging
union seals the willing deaths to new departures.

All opening the way to this day and the aisle of consent
opening before you now, like the sea of reeds parting
before the mosaic staff, disclosing the sea- walled,
dry shod, fish flapping, seaweed strewn path - down
which you travel into the promised estate, that honeyed
confederacy, and your first babe's milk suck and tender nuzzle.

The slave drivers will pursue you, have no doubt, with
their whips of injunction and chariots of chariness,
but always be ready to let the sea close over them
and their false gods of order and idols of prudence.
You were drawn by grace to this wedding of generousness
where your hearts will be broken, but what could be better?

Adrian G R Scott

A Moment In Time

Just one moment – like any other?
No, a tiny portion of time when
something unexpected opens up
before you.
A phone call, bringing news
of the ending of a life.
The speaker falling over herself
to report the final hour,
as though framing it in words
would bring some reality,
some relief, after the long
hours, days, months of caring for
her partner as his life
ebbed away before her.
And at that very moment,
a text announces its
arrival with a ping to
herald the birth of a grandchild
after the long night's
labouring and waiting.
Something opened up within me,
like the sun bursting out
from behind a cloud,
or two great oceans
meeting in explosive confrontation,
vying for position,
pushing against each other.
Turning from farewell tears
to welcome smiles,
the pain of losing a treasure,
and the joy of finding it again.
The moment when darkness

turns to light.
The utter beauty of it,
the two events bringing
a completeness, a reality,
that cannot be explained.
Something deep revealed that
words cannot express.
Welcome and farewell.
Losing and finding.
Dawn and dusk.

Jacky Stride

Secrets

They are known only to me,
in the deep, hidden soul,
held apart, held close,
barred to inspection.

The world requires access,
disclosure, transparency,
revelation of minutia
to demonstrate trust.

Is all unveiling good?
Some may be hurt, damaged
by openness, in a spate
of self-indulgent divulgence.

Yet a secret safeguarded
by deception and lies
corrodes and disrupts
a longed for intimacy.

My inner struggle debates
the desire to be fully known
against the need to guard
that never spoken shame.

Do I keep the drawer locked,
on the squirreled away past,
to protect another from
unnecessary embarrassment?

Some secrets cannot be shared.
Buried in my own darkness
they are never forgotten, but
let them rest in peace now.
The peace of silence.

Val Dawson

Chance To Move On

Part of me just wants to pack it all in, like the friend of my childhood, who'd grab the board game he was losing at and chuck it all over the floor, as he stormed off home.

Except I can't hang myself in here, as they took the boot off me at the start; so I've got no laces. Just this small bright orange cell, the obligatory three barred window and infrequent visiting.
It's like one of those walks, where your parents drag you round the countryside, and then come out with, 'If you don't start enjoying yourself, you'll be grounded for the rest of the week.'
Well, that visit didn't last long, did it? 'Just passing through', 'on a roll,' he said. It's alright for some with their very own home and income. The freedom that money brings, hey? I've got nothing to my name.

Tragedy from the word go, just two wrong moves, that was all it took. I should never have listened to the others; 'always take chances' they said, and look where it got me. Meanwhile, them lot, get to swan around wherever the wind blows, travelling, earning, buying stuff and on the off chance, then once in a while, they find the time to drop by and pay me a visit.

Don't get me wrong, it's great to see them, but all they talk about is life on the outside. Man I resent that. Celebrating birthdays, and do they ever remember mine? Buying property, visiting each other. Life's just so unfair. Oh yeh, they try to console me with 'It's the way the dice falls mate!' and 'You were just in the wrong place at the wrong time.'

When I get out, I'll show them a thing or two. I have dreams, I can save up and get a house of my own. His house sounded good. Cost a fortune mind, all green apparently, although was he talking about the colour or did he mean environmentally? Still living bang next to a station can't be much fun.

No I just want out, no more chances for me, I'll tell you.

Last time I got out, I was straight back in here. They all laughed so hard, it nearly upset everything. Some group of friends they are.

I could just get up and leave. I feel like I'm in here for their benefit, giving them the chance to get on in life, and take every opportunity that comes their way. There'll be nothing left for me when I get out, just that old brown house that nobody wants. The last visitor said as much, 'I left that for you' he said laughing, 'thought you'd like it!' Yeah really funny.

Just one more appeal. If I don't get a double this time, it'll cost me fifty quid to get out!

Andy Wilcock

Happy New Year

Out with the Old
In with the New
10 9 8 7 6 5 4 321
Big Ben chimes, the New Year has begun
imperceptible, intangible?

Will sadness suddenly disappear in a flash
to be replaced by joy and happiness?
Will illness and poverty be banished by the ticking of the clock?
In that one second
What has changed – anything?
Out with the old
In with the New

Happy New Year,
Happy New year
Jules Holland on TV
Music, smiles and laughter
Is all a veneer, a deception
a pretence that all is well?
Expectations are high, or appear to be

For most, more of the same
Same old ...same old....
and if not, all will surely be well this year,
Some stay 'til midnight and later
to greet the year with first footing friends and a piece of coal.
Others creep to bed with feigned indifference
to escape the hollowness of meaningless celebration

Happy New Year,
Happy New Year
How will tomorrow be different?

Somewhere a new life will be entering the world

Elaine Curl

Escape

Disarray! Floor strewn with petals, scattered from the pot plants; dirty waste on the table, a climate of agitation.
The wee siskin madly flaps his wings, repeatedly bashing his head against the big panes of glass, longing to fly into that world of freedom.

I move into the conservatory.
Trapped in this prison, and terrified of my presence, he thrashes around wildly, denuding the geraniums of more petals, and thudding against the glass time and again falling back and striving up. I step back and wait.

At last his frantic efforts defeat him. He drops onto the ledge, and lies there, heart pounding, exhausted.

I move gently towards him: 'It's alright. Don't be frightened. I've come to free you'. Resigned, with no more than a feeble flap of his wings, he now allows me to pick him up.

There in my hand he nestles, and I delight in his vulnerability. I revel in his beauty; the splendid gold and green, the intricate detail of his feathers, his little bright eyes, his beating heart, his softness against my skin.
'I love you little bird.'

Carefully I carry him outside with me; out from restriction, into this big airy, world of spaciousness and plenty; where he truly belongs.
He flies free.

Jane Lander

Self-Discipline

The Spirit is willing but the flesh is weak
I haven't been to bed early this week

Guilt lurks in my early-morning wardrobe
I wear him badly, his hems drag along the floor
Joy runs out through the holes in his pockets
Bank statement leans threateningly across the cornflakes
To remind me of my spiritual overdraft

The Spirit is willing but the flesh is weak
I've forgotten the promises made last week

Thank God the road to Hell *isn't* paved with good intentions
If it was, I would complain to the Council
Sue God, because the stones were uneven
And I tripped over and hurt myself
Watched my sweet-wrapped dreams turn soggy in the gutter

The Spirit is willing but the flesh is weak
There's a good late-night film on the telly next week

Waiting in ambush like a gang of muggers
I shall rise from black-eyed sleep with a bruised ego
Trail sheepishly down to the breakfast table to make a statement
My desk-sergeant wife will blame me in a 'told-you-so' kind of way
How many times did she tell me not to walk that unlit street
And to carry a video for protection?

My statement will turn into a confession
Written in Lamb's blood
But I fear the pen might run out
One of these mornings...   *Simon Copley*

Preston Sands Beach

Two deckchairs and a picnic rug
Declare our right of occupancy
-albeit temporary –
on a plot of sand called
Preston Sands Beach.
Bags and shoes
discarded roughly,
jostle for prime position
in the shadow-space
between chair
and soft, cool sand.
Towels pile up
on rug and chairs
with increasingly
dishevelled appearance
as the day wears on,
on Preston Sands Beach.

Looking out to sea
from my deckchair,
I take in all that my
temporary home
has to offer -
but, time and again,
I'm struck by the
busyness of the shoreline.
People walking, ambling,
running, surfing,
body-boarding,
playing, sitting;

seemingly resolved
on one thing:
to work hard at this task
called relaxing.

Taking time
from busy, stressful lives,
their intent is to silence
the voice of angst
as if placed in a box,
while they, in a bubble
called Holiday,
pretend that life is perfect;
couldn't be better;
wonderful;
dreading the day
when the bubble
bursts in a frenzy
called 'Going Home'.

Janice Speddings

Living With Your Depression

Why is my heart so old?
Time after time
raging nights catch
at the heels
of mild-mannered days
with restless dreams
of aching, forsaking.

And all too soon,
all too soon,
you'd gone.

I didn't move
to say good-bye.
Habituated,
I barely turned
to catch your eye.
Found solid words
on printed page,
more mesmerising
than your gaze.

And all too soon,
all too soon,
you'd gone.

Silently,
you slammed the doors.
I sensed the black dog
uncurl its claws.
Unreachable,
your silences scab over

so many promises,
that once spoken,
now picked away,
lie broken.
Whispers through keyholes
hold me hostage.
So do I wait?
Do I wait?
Do you miss me at all?
In your ivory tower
with padded walls?
Do I stand at the doors
and knock with love,
weary but resolved
to help you through?

By God, lost soul,
By God, I do.

Jill Wagg

Possession

We have to build another tarmac stripe across the green land
Snaking from Birmingham to the northern motorway
Juggernauts and Mondeos, white vans and super-minis
Their activity to feed our prosperity, so we're told

In our way the River Anker, an inconsequential stream
Except in floods when water spreads across the valley floor
Our road needs beam and column to pass above
Ground lowered by colliers gnawing at the seams

In a previous age engineers in tall hats and moleskin
Followed the same stream with their iron highway
Now transformed into four steel ribbons
Hung about with gantries and copper wires
An artery

So this obstacle too must be bridged
No simple matter. The railwaymen
Must protect us from speeding trains of fatal impact
Which draw power from these copper wires
Where to touch means fried civil engineering operative

To lift our beams we must have possession of the site
Which orange coated railwaymen only grant
At dead of night when their demanding machinery
Rests between its regulated rushes across the counties

Tonight we leave the dry warmth of our portakabin
Out from the strip light brightness to the dark
Scrunching across damp gravel glistening in the light of the floodlights
Walking booted and in yellow jacket and hard hat

At the fence we meet the orange coats standing by their rails
Wait for a liturgy of procedures
Yes the track is blocked. Red flags in position and detonators placed
Now the isolation
Somewhere down the track a switch is thrown, documents are signed
The copper above now earthed to the rails by twisted wires
There will be no frying tonight

The stage is ours, without interruption,
Except that they have to pass an engineering train
At a particular time, they will tell us when
We have the possession

The abutments of our bridge stand waiting
Monolithic concrete pale floodlit against the dark
Gold midge swarms of drizzle drops
Illuminated in the floodlights
It's a soft night the Irish would say

Offstage dimly sits the great yellow crane
Spider-like on its outriggers
The inclined column of its jib
Disappearing upwards into the dark

Slowly it turns and a beam floats above into the light
The slings that hold it hanging from the unseen jib
Slowly, slowly it moves
It is so full of weight
We can do nothing quickly with the beam's smooth heaviness

But in time gloved hands guide its ends
With precise hand signals to the hidden driver
On to their landing places on the monoliths
It is always good to see that they actually fit

There are a good few of these beams to land tonight
Our yellow coats work with deliberation
As the structure grows
And there is the usual banter

A message from the guardians below
They have the train to pass
Headlights reflect off the steel rail ribbons
It grumbles to a halt while flags and detonators
(our protection) are removed and replaced

The loco stops for a moment
Engine boggler, bogglering on tickover
Behind, huge wagons with strange equipment
Blocking out the floodlights
While the orange coated ones
Exchange arcane information with the driver

Then we are cleared to resume our steady repetitions
Until at length the job is done
Everything is stowed and made secure
The crane jib drawn in and lowered rests silent
The site is tidy, the railwaymen are satisfied
The liturgy is reversed
And the possession is handed back

Back to the bright dry yellow light of the portakabin
The action is over
We feel heavy eyed as we make out reports
But the craic is always good on a possession

And the first train of the dawn rushes through
Beneath our bridge, just another fleeting blur
Half seen from the carriage's window   *Robin Dawson*

The Diggers

Like a surveyor, he studied the ground carefully. He paced up and down, examining certain spots with care. He rejected some, went back several times to others and eventually selected one small patch of ground. He circled round and round, just to be sure.

Like an archaeologist, he carefully marked out the boundaries of his chosen spot. Cautiously, at first, he began to remove the earth around it. Then his pace quickened and he began to dig in earnest.

Like a gardener, he worked with great concentration. It took a long time to excavate the place he had designated. He turned around a number of times during this process, dislodging some soil, and then apparently changing both his mind and the direction of his digging as he filled it back in and started again.

Like a gravedigger, his pace quickened as more and more earth was thrown up. Eventually, satisfied, he glanced all around him, turning his back on any possible onlookers.

Finally, furtively, like a cat burglar, he deposited a package in the hole and backed away.

Like a small child, he enthusiastically began to fill it in again, with little care as to whether the earth went back where it belonged or whether it went elsewhere. But the final result seemed satisfactory. He took one last look and walked off, casually. All that remained to be seen on the surface was a small mound where the ground had been disturbed.

And then, like a dog, the dog who shared the house with him shot out into the garden and immediately uncovered what his feline friend had so carefully secreted just moments before.

Ruth Grayson

Turning Fifty

Tonight, driving home in the dark,
I follow a car down the dual carriage way to the traffic lights.
Two heads up front, nodding in conversation.
Suddenly, up pops a third, bang in the middle of the back seat,
bobbing about, a lively one this.
Can't be helpful to the driver.

All of a sudden, another head appears.
Were these back seat people grovelling for something on the floor?
Then another, like a jack-in-the-box set free.
What's going on in there?
Back seat discipline is not what it should be.
Then a fourth. Eh?

The traffic slows for the lights, and I pull up behind.
Even in the orange street light I can see more clearly…bald,
uniform, patterned.
Reality dawns as the front seaters turn and wrestle the heads.
50!…50!…50! they announce, as they bob and sway and float free.

Desperate efforts to arm-lock the escaping celebration,
To contain it in a flurry of black plastic.
The lights change, the driver lets go and the car jolts forward
A silent cheer erupts from the back seat
As the dancing crowd is joined by the final escapees, a heart and a star
And the car transforms to a party-on-wheels.

I turned 50 a short while ago.
Mixed feelings, still 20 in my head
But maths adding up to middle age.
Yet more limiting than TV's preoccupation with the young
Were the events going on before this landmark

The suffocating frustration of providing for the impossible
A long overture to the crush of double bereavement
For a long time it felt like my stomach was full of concrete

But now, by some unseen magic, this dead weight is transformed
I didn't see how or when
But like that first escaping balloon
Something in me is lifting me up
And I feel I'm beginning to float free at last

A friend grins at me
'I've never said this to anyone before, but you're looking younger'
A silent cheer erupts inside me
I'm not just imagining it!
50!..50!..50!...I bob and sway and float free.

Jane Truman

For Farah's Passing

Read at the funeral of Farah, August 2014

We stand,
staring down the barrel of a mystery;
an immersed in life,
treasuring wife,
mother of two sons,
her birth immediately
familial and sisterly,
her frontier breaking,
her welcome to the broken,
her hearth home making,
all too shortly done.

We hold,
the riveting shock of loss, a wrench;
taking us apart,
breaching the heart,
impossible to explain,
keening sobs that drench,
no condolence can quench
the tears that sting,
as the mourning gongs ring,
the sounds circling
with strains in sorrows vein.

We speak,
in ways that flow, issuing
from secret places,
stories flow in remembered faces,
we need to tell and retell our grief
until the telling takes the trauma,

transforming full stop into comma,
absence and recalling
are her presence now,
her departure into what we can only guess
her life's energy that beautiful prow
crossing the outer reef.

We take our leave,
as you have of us, in this veil-thin space;
carrying you as you carried us,
unsteady steps, we strain to adjust,
to this hard leave-taking,
that sculpts a new creation
lives framed by separation
yet I sense a holding in this fierce embrace
beyond the sum of all our parts
the mystery we stare down;
that the leave-taking of all human hearts
can come to be a new-dawn-waking.

Adrian G R Scott

Re-Acquaintance

On Saturday, I met myself again.
Slipped away in the early morning
to a place of space and breathing
escaping the plainness of my life.
Leaving the rush and urgent
pull of needs and musts to
meet with nature, air, earth,
and vast, sweeping river.
My senses slowed and came awake,
resting but full of the real
energy of life in all its fullness.
All of life, it seemed, on the cusp
of some huge explosion.
Fecund and ripe, the trees
trembled with anticipation
of bursting into glory.
Flowers shyly shining with
new colour, and......
the river. Ah, the river –
slipping by, dangerous, yet playful,
inviting and powerful
source of life and
taker of life.
I sat, and listened and watched
and came alive again,
safely back in my own skin.

Jacky Stride

Light

I place my chin on the rest
fix my eyes on the light ahead
hold the switch in my hand
and press to acknowledge the flash.

There's a spark, a flicker, a glimmer
now up, now down, one side or the other
nearby and far, just on the edge.
They call it peripheral vision.

I'm being tested, so what do I see?
I focus ahead on the yellow beam
but respond to the red pricks
registering their presence with a press.

I wonder how many I am missing
what sparks do I let fly by unnoticed?
Once, she was my strong central light
revealing to me so much of life.

Now, she is among these ones on the edge
a flicker that says 'see Homi',
a flash that encourages me to risk,
a twinkle that says 'no' to fear.

She knew how to live differently
and loved that into being in so many others;
Always shining the light of possibility
for me and them, then fanning the flame into life.

Now, when a new idea begins to glimmer
out there and I begin to hesitate, hold back
she sparkles her quirky, magic dust,
her flair, into my 'could be' world.

I could focus my life, as instructed,
solely on that straight-ahead beam
but I would miss those flashes of hope
that glitter even in the darkness of loss.

Her joyful light can guide me, to say 'Yes' only
to the best, as she stretched life, challenging
all it hurled at her. Now in death her wisdom
may shimmer obliquely near or obtusely far.

But as the sun does not die, even in the darkest night
or behind the blackest storm cloud,
but will shine again, so she, Rachel, sparkles again,
if only I will notice, in my peripheral vision.

Val Dawson

A Happy Christmas, By Kevin Aged 13

The familiar smells and sounds of Christmas morning: A musty blanket, disinfectant and someone's singing echoing down the corridor, to the jingling keys.

I'm trying not to move on this hard bed, avoiding the inevitable peeling feeling I'll get as my back separates from the thin plastic mattress, leaving my sweaty back to go rapidly cold.

Bang! The thud against the door makes me jump. 'Do you want the toilet?' John's voice suddenly booming from just outside. 'Yeh', I shout, and the door swings open to the sound of more jingling keys. There's my wheels for a trip down to the toilets. Ben is in number three as we were lifted together. He was the one pushing me down the high street at the time: Not our best getaway. 'Happy Christmas Ben!' I shout, as I wheel past. 'Ho! Ho! Ho!' echoes back through the door and down the corridor. John laughs and asks if Father Christmas has been. 'No he's locked up in number 4, the pedo' Ben shouts back.

All it took was three cans each, two bricks and crash, Ben was in through WH Smith's window, with the alarm ringing in our ears.

8 O'clock, Christmas Eve and no court till Boxing Day.

'Here they come', Ben shouted climbing back through the window. He dumped two magazines, three DVDs and a calculator in my lap. 'What's the calculator for, yeh nob?' I shouted over the distant ringing alarm and fast approaching sirens behind us. Ben looked back over his shoulder as we sped down the street. 'Look out!' I cried as my wheels hit a bench. I left the chair, slid along the seat and off the other end, crashing into a bin. Still you can't get paralyzed twice, although the last crash did involve a 'T.W.O.C.ed[1]' car and a lamppost. Funny the police were chasing us then as well.

Well it's worked and here we are, second year on the run, free from where we belong: No unpredictable, random, violent, drunken, arguing parents and no empty space under the tree where Father Christmas won't have been.

At least this will be a laugh, Christmas dinner, cake and a cracker each. 'Even the guards wore paper crowns last year Ben' I thought 'Safe' and then shout 'Happy Christmas Ben!

Andy Wilcock

───────────

[1] T.W.O.C. is the police term for stolen car. 'Taken Without Owner's Consent'. TWOC is also used between Young Offenders, Police, Social Workers and Solicitors.

Where Have All The Young Men Gone?

Where have all the young men gone?

Who thronged our cornered streets and pubs and drank their booze?

Played football on a Wednesday in our parks,

married their sweethearts, for love and larks

And came to church to fill the pews?

And sang

And laughed all the way to Scarborough in the Sunday-School charabanc?

While they bank-holidayed on that last summer day,

bearing a name that none of them had heard

A town, a million miles away,

saw a malicious butterfly flap its wings

A fanatic, terrorist or freedom fighter, according to how you view these things,

whatever, murderous chaos theory put into bloody practice, changed their lives for ever in the space of a shot

A starting pistol, crackling round the world, for a race of twenty million souls towards their glory and the guns

Their only victory garland: blood-red flowers swaying in a Flanders field

Survivors - in name alone, left their broken souls in louse-infested trenches

And dragged their broken bodies home, to charity, dull and dozing, on cold park benches

Widows found wartime work, instead,

but wages only put their bread

upon a lonely table, Broken alone,

unshared, an unconsummated communion in an empty bed

A million tragic chapters make this Empire's story

Book-marking time to lose its place on history's page

Once in the pink, now straining to a blood-red high-tide upon the map of time

Economic laws of precious metal destroyed the works of man as surely as its baser brothers tore his flesh

And treasure, turned to tools for torture, could make nothing more concrete than a fragile peace

Faith buried in Picardy and Piedmont, came also to Palestine, land of her birth, to die

God's voice grew silent, His living pages gathered dust in a million graves, where dead ears could not hear His call

To go into all the world and preach

But the world came to our door to teach

a humbled church to bow in silence, to listen, to kneel in penitence, Her throne to yield,

while other, stranger voices claimed this their home and took the field

War memorials trumpet no more past glories of earth's proudest empire

But speak instead of sacrificial stories and lives laid down, and tested in the flame-thrown fire

Do we reach backwards to those smiling, marching boys, only in the fading notes of our last posts?

Or do their ghosts

step forward here and sit in empty chairs

And whisper in our memory-slipping ears of what just might have been?

For ten young men, re-enrolled, re-mustered on each chapel wall, will not grow old as we that are left...

But neither shall age their twenty unborn children weary: they shall not, with us, grow old in wisdom...

Nor the years their fifty grandchildren condemn: they also shall not grow old with ours...

Nor one hundred of another generation receive and learn new faith from Sunday hours

A congregation crucified, in their own misguided Passion

Upon the wire of Passchendaele, will not rise again to speak and pass it on

But can life that shall endless be, from foreign ground still blossom red?

For if the seed that fell into that shell-torn ground should die and yield a hundred-fold, what then?

Is it at the going down of a Good Friday sun, and in the dead of faithless night that we now remember them?

Or in the morning? In the dawning resurrection of a new world,

Where banners of the Prince of Peace are now, upon the still-contested earth, at last, unfurled?

Simon Copley

The Picture

Which picture, which picture?
Images flicking through my mind
As if through unwanted facebook messages
Spinning round as a ball on a roulette table

Passing the great masters
The endless exhibitions both near and far
Large and small
With only a passing glance
At those specially selected for personal possession
Where will the ball stop?

Which picture, which picture?
How will I know which to choose
Which is THE one
When the wheel stops spinning
And the ball is still?

This picture, this picture
A simple child like drawing
Pinned on a wall
No golden frame
The canvas a sheet of white paper

No subtle blending of colours for this artist
Rather primary colours of yellow, red and black
The medium crayon and coloured pencil
No attention to technique
No specially designed lighting to enhance the scene
Stark electric light overhead.

Not the artistic skill which halts the spinning wheel
But the graphic content.
Stick-like figures, pin men
With speech bubbles issuing from their mouths
Reminiscent of a comic strip or cartoon.

But this is no cartoon
A large deep rectangular container is centre stage
Filled with water
The stick-like figures are crawling up the side,
One is face down in the water
Others are lying prostrate on the floor nearby
Calling for help.

The 'artist'...
A survivor of the bomb dropped on Hiroshima
His memories of the unquenchable thirst
And aftermath.
Images which will haunt me forever
This picture, this picture

Elaine Curl

Secret

Behind the willow trees it lay, in the dried-up ditch, overgrown with ivy: in *our garden*. Nightly, from my bed, my child-imagination tortured me with dread of policemen, and prison. The police knew everything, and they would find anything they were looking for. They would discover the secret that only Pam and I knew. How I wished we had left it where it was – or at least anywhere other than in my garden. It wasn't even buried very deeply. Pam lived away up the road. I would be accused as a criminal, and I would have to face this all on my own.

Perhaps we were too influenced by Enid Blyton's books. Pam and I were so eager to solve 'mysteries'. We searched for clues in the ditches either side of the busy by-pass road, just an orchard and field away from the bottom of the garden. Bits of paper and other rubbish (probably thrown from car windows), were all objects of our scrutiny, and subjects of the stories we imagined of suspicious events and happenings.

On this particular day we were searching the dusty hedge bottom amongst the litter, devising gruesome interpretations of any writing we found. Then, there, half hidden by the grass and weeds, we discovered it: a bulky sack, tied at the neck. This was real stuff! Well, we couldn't just leave it there. The criminal had obviously put it there temporarily, and would be back for it. We had to move it.

It was rather heavy. Between us, we pushed it through the rails of the fence, climbed over, dragged it across the field, avoiding the horse-pats, and up through the orchard, past the hen-house. What should we do with it? We had to hide it somewhere, out of the way. So, opening the orchard gate, and heaving the bulk across the lawn, we flung it under the willow trees. Pulling aside the rampant ivy of decades, we burrowed down a little into the earth, pushed the bundle underneath, and covered it over again.

So that was that. That was that until nighttime. Alone in my little bed in the dark attic I kept revisiting the scene of the burial. Obviously the detectives would come and trace the crime to us, or actually to *me*, on my own, because it was in *my* garden. I couldn't tell anyone. (I knew from when I had stolen some loose change from the ledge in the dinning room, that if I was threatened with the police, I was on my own.) So the dread lingered, and sleep eluded me.

How much pain can be caused by a secret – the Mystery of the Murderous Poacher – the secret of a bag of dead bunnies in the ditch.

Jane Lander

Scottish Island Swim

We plan, we pack
We set out
We joke, we chatter
We arrive
We choose our spot and we stake our claim

We go down to inspect the sea
We discuss
We paddle
We reconsider
We create excuses
We eat lunch

We revisit our first intentions
We recommit
We inspect the sea again
We discuss
We theorise that sand will warm sea
We decide to wait for the tide

We get changed slowly
We debate the best place for towels
We arrange and rearrange our things
We agree the sea is colder in June
We shouldn't take risks
We go down just to look

We dip a toe
We shudder
We dip our ankles
We laugh
We dip our knees

We yell
We stand wobbling and giggling for an eternity
We plunge, we gasp
We can't breathe
But we can scream
We strike out, jerky and tense
We hop, ungainly, foot to foot
We recover from shock
We smile

We relax, we float
We swim, we splash
We glory in the moment
We see with wide opened eyes
We feel with renewed touch
We hear with keen ears
And we know the moment fully

We splash our way out
We run zig zags up the beach
We jump for warmth and for joy
We towel down and lose knickers and socks
We force clothes over wet limbs
We collapse, damp and satisfied

We sip hot tea and whiskey
We share cake, crisps and chocolate
We chatter teeth and conversation
We warm up and we quieten down

We linger as long as we can
We amble our return
We join friendship without words
We're content   *Jane Truman*

Easter Party

'Companion' from Latin meaning one who eats bread with another

The colour of the air
changes when you walk in.
Light softens and dampens
stark peacock hues.

The rising and falling of breaths
of strangers and friends,
the pulsating of their bloods,
around the melody
mark time until the end.

Eyes flick quickly,
not meeting your welcome,
not begging your pardon,
as you weave through the room.
And I smash the wineglass from your hands,
watch hell-bent, ruby drops
trickle and pool on the floor.

'Mine,' I said.
'Not yours to take,
so mine to break.'

Then, I saw your feet were bare,
studded with shards of glass
and blinding red beads.
'Companion,' you offered,
reaching out.
'Walk with me.
I have your pain.'   *Jill Wagg*

A Moment Of Anxious Possibilities

Barriers of metal across Sheffield streets
tell of roads that are closed: so shoppers beware!
Police in attendance on high alert
waiting and watching, noting and clocking
who was around and why were they there?

Trouble converging from opposite sides,
from doctrines conflicting, with hostile intent;
two groups displaying their freedom to march,
regardless of peace, of justice or right,
they turned up in force, their anger to vent.

My bus travelled West Street, unimpeded its route -
past roads I have walked down without any thought.
But the sight of police with bullet-proof vests
caused fear and anxiety deep in my soul, while
questions of 'what if…' rose uninvited, unsought.

What if the police couldn't hold back the hate?
What if the violence spun out of control?
What if our safeguarded streets became places
where allegiance to causes dictated safe passage?
My mind was benumbed while images unrolled.

But with West Street, police and barriers behind me
I gratefully let all my anxious thoughts go:
Those questions, too deep for coffee shop thoughts,
I waved to my friend and thought light-hearted things –
'cos it couldn't possibly happen in the place I call home…..?

Janice Speddings

Mary's Secret

Everybody knows my secret, because everybody knows my song.
But have they realised that I only sang once?
When I, myself, first got the news?
The rest is silence.
I had to keep a secret.
A secret that was too great to tell for over thirty years.

My heart is overflowing.
Who would ever believe me?
Maybe God did choose me well.
No one could possibly guess my secret.
Me, the lowliest of the low, mother of His Son?

My heart rejoices!
An angel came last night and told me
What to expect in nine months' time.
I've spoken to my cousin
For I know my secret is safe with her.
After all, she has a secret of her own.
But what shall I tell my fiancé?
He surely won't understand.
It's not just that he's a man, it's also
That he simply won't believe it isn't my fault.

My heart is breaking.
He says he want to finish with me.
I know I shouldn't have told him,
But it won't be long before it begins to show
And then things would be even worse.
I don't suppose even my parents will want me back.
I've brought disgrace on them
Although I don't know how.

My heart is full.
Joseph has changed his mind.
Apparently he had a dream too,
And God told him my secret
So I don't have to.
But how can we live with this?
Who will believe us?
I don't think we'll be able to tell anyone else.
Ever.

My heart is searching for answers.
About those shepherds.
Why did they come?
Why were they the first to be chosen
To see the son of God?
They are even poorer than I am.
Yet they have gone on their way rejoicing,
As if their lives are suddenly worth living.

My heart is aching.
I long to speak out
And say: 'This is my son!
My son, who has healed you!
My son, who has fed you!
My son, who has taught you!
My son, who you do not recognise
Is also the son of God!'

My heart is broken.
His pain, his anguish, his sorrow is killing me too.
I will never, never recover from this.

My heart is bursting.
My son – risen from the dead!
He is alive!
Whom can I tell?
Does anyone else alive still know
That I, Mary, the lowliest of the low
Am the mother of God's son?

I've kept quiet for too long
And I can't contain myself any longer.
Would that Luke believe me?
Maybe I will tell him.
He's a doctor.
My secret will surely be safe with him.

Ruth Grayson

Bug Hotel

Something was happening at the bottom of the garden!
Stag the beetle watched from his hiding place.

The family who lived in the house at the top of the garden were very busy.
They were carrying wood and leaves, bark and bamboo, sticks and
stones, cardboard, straw and hay.
Then they started to build.

Stag scuttled a bit closer.
'It' got bigger and bigger.
He couldn't see the top.

When they had finished, he heard the man say 'Well done
everyone, let's go into the house for a drink'.

Stag waited until it was very quiet. He slowly crept nearer and
nearer and crawled up to the top of the pile.
A sign hung at the top.
He read 'Bug Hotel'
'Bug Hotel?'
He thought for a while.
'I'm a bug – it must be for me!'

He started to explore.
There were lots of nooks and crannies, big holes and little holes,
sunny spots and damp dark gloomy gaps.
He found some dead wood.
'Stupendous' shouted Stag.
'I could live here. I must go and tell the others'
Off he went.

He found Sammy Spider, Suzy centipede, Lucy lacewing, Willie
woodlice, Lily ladybird, Bizzy bee and Millie pede.
'Come with me' he said 'I've found a great place for us – it's called
Bug Hotel'
'What's a hotel?' Willie wondered.
'Come and see' said Stag.

So off they went to explore.
Some of them crawled. Some of them flew.
'Buzzootiful bamboo' buzzed Bizzy 'perfect place for my bed'
'Wow' said Willie when he saw the bark and he crept underneath.
Millie and Suzy followed him and snuggled into little gaps.
'Lovely' Lucy lacewing laughed 'I've found a bed in a bottle just
for me' and she settled into the crinkly cardboard she found inside.
Lily ladybird lay down on some leaves.

Stag scuttled around and was happy.
'This is a safe place for us all' he thought 'and there is still space
for lots of other creatures'
He wondered who else might come and join them....but that's
another story

Elaine Curl

What Is Man That You Are Mindful Of Him?

Am I more than what I own, the trinkets stacked up round my home
Dusty fool's-gold carriage clocks? A drawer of Auntie's birthday socks?
Or am I more than what I've done, achieving like my father's son?
Certificates within a frame, a video of my quart-hour fame?
Cracked image in an attic album, brought out in the Christmas sun?
A cardboard box of boyhood toys, an ever-fainter memory-noise?

Or am I found in what I say, far too much 'Truth', too little 'Way'?
Am I my yesterdays compiled when everything was going great?
Or a thoroughly post-modern child, preyed upon by fear and hate?
Am I talents, neatly labelled, user-friendly, stacked in line?
Or political, my motions tabled?
Or theologically defined?
Or what I've eaten (fat and greasy), chocolate to feed an army?
The sum of thoughts, deep, yet uneasy
And sometimes slightly barmy?

Or like James 'doo-dah' in that film? Oblivious to my 'wonderful' life?
The sum of my effect on others? Only <u>dead</u>, missed by my wife?
Oh what I wear - a Benetton? Or where I live - an Anglo-Celt?
Am I more than where I've been and seen and heard and felt?

Am I the hero deep inside or still the coward on the screen?
Am I what is yet to come or all the things I might have been?
Am I the 'me' I find inside, although, to me, an ugly sight?
Am I that contradictory child who cowers, fearful, in the light?

Sometimes I'm the centre and sometimes I'm the sun
And sometimes I'm a nobody, but then, the <u>only</u> one
Planets circle round my will then pass without a glance
My life has colour every day
But then it's just a chance

I think therefore I am, I know, but don't know what to think!
I'm evolution's pinnacle – Confusion's missing link.

Simon Copley

The Peleton

Yer in Yorkshire, lad, Wharfedale, top end
Ther's a thousand souls and forty thousand sheep in the parish
The dale is straight, steep sides in pale limestone terraces
Straight stone walls form fields
Irregularity is found in villages
Higgledey piggledey collections a stone houses
Connected by a road that twists and buckets up the valley
Between stone walls at once sinuous and threatening.

This morning is grey and misty
Rain has been siling down all night
Rattling on the canvas of little tented towns
Sprung up along the valley

Out of the tents come cyclists
Here to watch the Grand Depart
At dawn the road was deserted
Now there is a stream of riders
In their best lycra
Cycling with contented deliberation
Along a road which, for once, is solely theirs
Up the course to find the best spec
Maybe on the cote de Cray

There is something like quiet joy about
This is the cyclist's day
They have the road to themselves
They stream on up the valley
Club riders, friends, families, kids
Some stopping momentarily
Mystified by a flock of yellow sheep

In the villages decked with bunting,
Hung with yellow bicycles
The steady stream is applauded
Joy shared, mutual appreciation

We go down to the village
And find a bank above the road
Where it swoops down on a bridge over the river
Curving past the filling station and the public toilets
To jink left over a hump back bridge
And shimmy between the Blue Bell and the Racehorses

The sun is out now
Regulation puffy white clouds in a blue sky
Green fields and lush trees
Yorkshire has put on its best today

Soon there is a stream of official vehicles
Gendarmes and police on motorbikes
Strange floats advertising drinks, banks and hotels
Everybody gets applauded, that's how we feel
Seems to go on a long time
But the sun is out and we are happy

Its quiet
Down the valley we see the helicopters
riding shotgun on the race
blue lights, more motorbikes
Three racers skim past
Another pause, more blue lights
The peleton is upon us

Like a strange creature alive with colour and movement
A creature is made of darting cyclists, silent,
Independent, yet acting as one, a rainbow shoal, human, quicksilver

The creature flows accommodating itself to the road's irregularities
Curving through the village, left and right over the bridges,
shimmying between the pubs
And it is gone

It was so beautiful and it is gone
There's a lump in my throat
Quietly the crowds of watchers disperse
I'll not see that again in my lifetime
We did 'em proud in Yorkshire, eh?

Robin Dawson

So Why Am I 'Tutting'?

The task in hand was going well. Half the border cleared in 40 minutes. Plants identified, roots avoided, weeds located and meticulously removed from deep down in the soil. Those uprooted now lay helplessly wilting in the sun.

Meanwhile, music and chattering hummed away in the distance, to the chink of glasses and bottles.

A tut was audibly heard, and he was curious to the reason. He knew where it had come from, but he wanted to know why. It can't have been the weed he'd just wrestled from the bed, or the muffled noise of the party, maybe it was the child, who that very moment, had appeared like a ghost from nowhere, momentarily becoming solid as she planted a heavy foot into the freshly broken soil before him? No he knew secretly, the answer to why he'd uttered the tut; it was the present, impending, nagging, gloom of responsibility.

Persistently he continued with his task, interrupted briefly by the stampede of enthusiastically, overdressed footprints across his freshly dug soil, but they evaporated into the background as quickly as they had appeared, allowing him to sink comfortably back into the oblivious bliss of his weeding.

Intermittently above the hum of the party, his name could be heard, called and the question asked, more than once, 'has anyone seen the bride's father?'

Andy Wilcock

Pembrokeshire Coast Path

Cliff and hillside splashed with gold,
While rivers of pink and white tumble
Down the banks and cling to the
Precipitous edge for dear life.
Puddles of violet and primrose
Catch me unawares.
Salt laden wind does its best
To halt my progress along
This ancient, life steeped coast,
While sea, looking so innocent,
Licks the kaleidoscope colours of the shore,
Then suddenly sucks away as if
Displeased with the taste.
Round the next headland and
The ocean, frustrated by the narrow
Space between land and island
Boils and rips its way in a
Treacherous tidal race.
Stripped of all power and strength
In this Celtic wonderland
I can but express my gratitude
For being held in such awesome beauty.

Jacky Stride

Now

The snail slowly glides its silvery way across the path. 'I can never really know what it is like to be you, snail. For I am me. Here at this moment we both are. You may or may not have purpose in where you are going, but the important thing is that you <u>are</u>. And I am.'

So also that rose. It can't move anywhere. It just blooms where it is planted, emitting its fragrance and stunning beauty. 'I didn't make you, rose. You are so other than me. And here you are. Once you were a bud, and I don't know what will happen to you in the future. The wonder is that you exist at this moment, and we can admire each other in our awesome being.

And I? What am I? I look at my hand, part of me. All my anxieties about my to-do list, all my memories of yesterday's pleasures and pains cannot alter the fact that in this moment I am, authorised by the Holder of it all. I open myself to the wonder of it all, and I rest in the Life that is unconditionally here, now.

Oh that I could more fully live that core nowness when the wind howls and a myriad tasks demand attention, and I feel low, and a pipe bursts, and there's a knock at the door. I still am.

Jane Lander

Three Angels

Three angels came to our door.
Death brought along his partner, Grief.
Only rarely and sadly does Death come without Grief.
And for us, they brought a third partner, Time.

Time did not stay Death's hand, but slowed it.
She worked grace and poise as she opened up an in-between place.
Not for us a brutal tearing, but a lingering, sweet-paced parting,
Gifting us room to be ourselves as we accepted Death as a house guest.

Death's steps around the house were measured and calm,
No sudden moves but still unstoppable progress.
As Death took from us, Grief took hold of us,
Gently at first, her full strength restrained by Time.

When she was ready, Time released Grief to press tighter,
The force of her grip alerted us to what Death was about,
Her embrace all muscle and bone, immovable and sharp,
Her unrelenting hold made us alive to the reality of Death's work.

And so we were ready when Death made his final moves,
Gifting one a quiet escape tunnel, the other a slow waltz.
Giving their last days a characteristic beauty.
And with their departure Death too slipped away from the door.

Grief and Time have stayed on with me.
Grief is a difficult lodger,
Overriding every moment and influencing every plan,
Consuming energy and sapping strength.

Time is not hurrying Grief away, but has become my wise guide,
Showing me how to settle with Grief, how to return her embrace,
Time and Grief together awake unexpected instincts in me,
Showing me how and when to move forward with the legacy of Death.

Jane Truman

The Disappointment Gene

When life seems like a chaotic chasm
filled with the dead dry, dry dead bones
of sadness and disappointment,
can a secure rope let down from above
haul one survivor to the surface,
even while another wrestles
with repeated frustration and anger
in the gorge below among the bones
of inherited abuse and disabling self-doubt?

Could a three-threaded cord hold firm,
bearing the weight of long held shame,
not once or twice but three times repeated?
This deadening burden, that needs to be
left to echo with the other bones
clings familiarly, hindering freedom
from the secret, so long buried
in darkness, that remains unnamed.

The rope still dangles, belayed firmly
to the tree above, its roots buried in deep earth.
To grasp the line, to call 'climbing'
seems impossible, with a heart hardened,
trust lost, through too many failures.
Now see, that flaccid thread has tautened
as if a weight descends the cliff. Yet fear hides
among the rattling skeletal mass.

But tears are washing these trembling bones,
as love comes down, hands and feet bleeding
from the cliff's sharp rocks and shared sorrow.
The rope wraps round the softening form

And unseen wings lift both upwards.
The past shame, named, is quietly discarded
in the ascent and falls among the tree's roots.
So hope may yet be passed down, an inheritance
for another survivor.
Flesh may cover her brittle bones too.

Val Dawson

Hunger

In England
Hunger said 'feed me' -
but Time said 'not yet';
Hunger said 'listen to me' -
but Body said 'go away';
Hunger said 'feel my pain' -
but Brain said 'It's mind over matter'.
Hunger persisted and grew louder
and Time said 'it's early, but ok';
Body said 'I've heard you'
and Brain said 'sometimes
you just have to give in'.
And Hunger was appeased.

In Africa
Hunger said 'feed me' -
and Time said 'I can't';
Hunger said 'listen to me' -
and Body said 'I'm sorry';
Hunger said 'feel my pain' -
and Brain said 'I feel it strongly'.
Hunger persisted and grew louder
and Time said 'I wish I could';
Body said 'I can't do anything'
and Brain said 'I am numb
with your burden'.
And Hunger cried silently.

Janice Speddings

A Meeting Of Waters

for Maggie and John on their Wedding Day

Far from here
That way!
A wellspring
Bubbled up,
Began to map
A tentative course.

And far from here
That way!
Another wellspring
Arose
To trickle a hesitant way.

And these two waters
Gathered and garnered
Depth and momentum,
Became two streams,
Stumbling, stubborning,
Carving courses,
Over and under,
Round and through
Stoney setbacks,
Brute boulders.
Tripping and hurtling
Down falls and fissures.
Meandering and seeming lost
At times,
But always running onward,
As best they could

Until
They Met
Here.

And
A river forms.

And from here,
Hear!
The rushes whisper
Joy!
Willows sigh
Joy!
Fish plash
Joy!
Birdsong spirals swoops
Joy!
Wildfowl bob
Joy!
Paws splash,
Tongues lap
Joy!
Skiffs skim
Fingers trail-trace
Joy!

And see the river's
Strength
As it pushes onward,
The life
It brings and carries,
Makes possible,
Always from now,
From here,
To

Far from here.
Where an open-handed estuary
Spreads wide its fingers,
Gives itself
At last!
Into a boundless sea.
Adventuring on
Far,
    Far,
        Far
           From here

Martina Towey

Talking Of The Bride

And talking of the bride…
Did you see her?
What a sight!
On her wet, wedding morning -
shimmering,
so gorgeous in white.
Wellies and wedding dress,
anticipating,
beautifully right.

And faith-filled vows
of love and life-long effort,
enthusiastically,
passionately said,
swept aside memories
of underwhelming mother mornings,
dragging her out of bed!

And my heart corkscrewed too,
as she turned -
enraptured, excited, delighted -
for that first marital kiss.
For in her shadow,
echoes of brides
still stand at the altar,
wedding in voluptuous bliss.

And now, day-ending dancing.
Have you seen her?
What a sight!

Joyful dancer, life enhancer,
Sparkling with delight.
Trusting him,
loving him,
my daughter – his wife.

Jill Wagg

Winter Walk

It's funny how the mood changes with the geology
Set out this morning in the long valley
Up the steep walled track behind Kettlewell
White walls and white track climbing a green slope
Horizontal ribs of Great Scar limestone
Fluffy clouds with patches of blue
A light breeze unlike the wind of yesterday
That had stalked the top of Great Whernside like an animal
It was a smiling morning
I was out testing my knees
Taking them out for a few days
To try them on long walks
The doctor had told me the cartilage was shot
You are getting old Mr Dawson
But the Coast to Coast is on my bucket list
The track followed the rising ridge
Up into the Millstone Grit
Now black acid soil, rank brown grass, wet peat
The path was rough and soggy
I'm not as nimble as I used to be
No tripping lightly up here, a long, long way from the road
The sun had gone, grey clouds closed in
Slopes above were streaked with snow
I had a powerful feeling
I was isolated and alone, but not alone
It was only me, but I was not alone
This was serious, it was real, but I was not alone
It's good to know that when you are alone, you are not alone

Robin Dawson

Welsh Non-Conformity

Welsh non-conformity
Plumps for uniformity
Now a dying breed
We let others take the lead
Baton-dropping grace
In the denomi-National relay race
Sticking to morality
With middle class finality
Wearing a hat
Is where it's at
Not radical, respectable
A pacified receptacle
Ever so faithful, to the wrong things
Holey woodworm, never-full buildings
Doesn't matter what the preacher said
He can juggle
Blow bubbles
Even stand on his head
Provided he's not too long
If he is, the sinner
We can sandwich him between hymns
Tear his sermon limb from limb
With our joint at Sunday dinner
And kiss the Lord goodbye with a so-familiar song.

Simon Copley

Sanctioned By The Heart

For the Wedding of Rachel and Ray, June 2014

What is it that brings and binds us together?
How does one life catch the fragrance of a
kindred spirit in another's passing waft?
Are there kindly angels directing our path
so that a momentous conjunction springs
passionately from an unplanned encounter?

What takes possession of our rationality
and leads us to that intoxicating coupling?
From whence comes the readiness to forsake
all others and cleave to one mortal life, as if
all our future happiness depended on it?
Is it just a genetic shelter for our children?

Can we reduce all this passion to a biological
necessity, spiraling DNA looking to survive?
Or rather does the sudden scent of Jasmine
sweeping across an Umbrian terrace come
from some other incantation, the movement
of great forces disguised in ordinary garb?

Some sweep into marriage within months
of this first heady cocktail of connection.
But you, you have waited many years to make
this final vowaging of your interleaving callings.
Your rings, the work of both your hands will pass
through the blessing palms of all here present.

This is an act of faith, faith in your accumulated
children's journeying, faith in the love that was
birthed on a summer's solstice, longest day of
light's enduring. Faith in the unfathomable hand
binding you together, faith in this second marriage
not sanctioned by state or country, but by the heart.

Adrian G R Scott

The Rivelin Writers

In the 1930s a group of miners from Ashington in Northumberland met under the auspices of the Worker's Education Association to study Art Appreciation in their spare time. The Tutor soon realised that looking at slides of Renaissance art was not their cup of tea, so he encouraged them to make art instead. They became known as the Pitman Painters. My Father, born in Ashington in 1910, must have known some of these colliers/artists. Here in the Rivelin Valley (where we meet), between the wars, there was an artist's colony in the old corn mill; they painted scenes up and down the riverbanks. It seems fitting to call our contributors the Rivelin Writers, placing ourselves at the confluence of these two creative streams. Ordinary people recording, in our case on paper, the way we experience life in Sheffield and its hinterland.

Adrian G R Scott is the convener of the two groups, a poet and writer living in the Rivelin Valley; he has worked as a Community Development Consultant in South Yorkshire and in the field of Spirituality. He is currently engaged in a PhD in creative writing producing a collection of poems exploring the poetry of place and focused on Sheffield in South Yorkshire.

Ruth Grayson is a retired academic, who is discovering how to write for pleasure instead of writing for work. She is always amazed at the rich diversity of approaches taken by the other group members and is learning to think much more creatively about a wide variety of topics.

Elaine Curl I am retired. From an early age I enjoyed 'creative writing' but pressures of work and family life meant that I only occasionally wrote anything. I am not good at painting and writing is a way I can paint with words and explore my thoughts and feelings more deeply. I like the group because everyone is very encouraging and supportive whatever my efforts! Different topics are a challenge (often daunting initially) and having to meet the deadline of the group meeting is a discipline! I love listening to the contributions from others and look forward to the evenings we spend together enormously.

Jacky Stride I am a retired counsellor now offering my time for spiritual accompaniment of others, leading courses and days to encourage spiritual growth. I am also a grandmother of 5 lovely grandchildren who all live here in Sheffield so I have the joy of spending time with them, and I also love working on our allotment and growing vegetables and fruit. I am unconfident of my skills as a writer, but whenever I do manage to get away for some space on my own – perhaps on a retreat – I like to express myself in poetry. These are nearly always poems celebrating the beauty and wonder of the natural world, which is where I find my own spiritual peace.

Jane Lander Retired from physiotherapy, much of my time is now occupied with spiritual accompaniment, gardening, walking, retreat-giving, time with friends, and running a Quiet Garden where people can enjoy space to be. From the age of 17, I have written a journal almost every day, finding this a tremendous personal help. Over recent years I had wondered about joining a writing workshop, or something. When Adrian started this group I was eager to join, and I find it supportive, creative and affirming.

Val Dawson Coming to writing later in life I am finding it an invaluable way of exploring both the personal and universal aspects of human life. The group provides a wonderful way of cross-examining my attempts at this, in a totally unthreatening and accepting atmosphere.

Janice Speddings I have worked as a Counsellor since 1989 but retrained as a Spiritual Director several years ago. I no longer take counselling clients, preferring to concentrate on my spirituality work which I like to approach creatively: writing, painting, crafting all find a place in my work and my play. A few years ago I decided to take a distance-learning diploma in creative writing and being part of Adrian's writing group enables me to continue indulging in my passion. Married for over 40 years with 2 adult daughters, a son-in-law and a cat, writing, reading, painting and crafting offer relaxation, challenge and a chance to let the world go by.

Robin Dawson I am retired. I used to write long reports. How my company could design gravel road in the back end of nowhere or a motorway in this country. How, now that we had designed the road the builders were making a bit of a pigs ear of it, and we had to say whether they deserved bit more money. Not very poetic. So when I retired I thought I might try writing poems about stuff that people think is not very poetic. Although when you look at it through my eyes it is. Adrian's group is a good group for trying things out like that.

Jill Wagg Despite having a supposedly 'empty nest', I juggle writing around a lovely, ever-expanding tribe and the impositions of chronic illness. Family, faith, health and a great deal of curiosity usually provide me with all the material I need.

Martina Towey I have always loved to write since I was a child - sub Enid Blyton school stories; 'soulful' teenage poetry; 'passionate' romantic novels! Now I am trusting my own unique voice more and more. I love the flint sparks of inspiration and energy that come from sharing works in progress in the writing group.

Jane Truman In my 'day job' I work with people preparing for a licensed role in church ministry. Writing is mainly confined to e-mails; meeting notes and helping people shape assignments on paper; important and fulfilling, but with definite conventions. I love the 'free range' writing shared among the group, getting away from rules and regulations and setting the imagination loose. I'm always pretty amazed when I pick up my pen as to what pops out, often unexpected but almost always helpful.

Andy Wilcock I'm married to Anne-Marie, and have two wonderful teenage girls. I took my Maths GCSE at the age of 24 and my English GCSE at 28 and recently I've been reading over 50 books a year. Over the past 15 years I have been a Youth Worker and Pastor. Through this work I developed a passion and skill for storytelling. It's lovely to be part of this encouraging writing group. They have really built up my confidence in writing, and in working with my ideas. Since I joined the group I've been able to write articles and stories for other situations.

Simon Copley I am a Minister in the United Reformed Church, previously in South Wales and now in South Yorkshire. I have also worked as a fundraiser for various local and national charities. In my 'spare time' I dabble in politics and ran for Parliament as an Independent in the 2012 Rotherham by-election. The writer's group is a great way to keep me earthed by listening to the personal experiences of others expressed in beautiful words. It also helps me let off steam, myself!

Printed in the United States
By Bookmasters